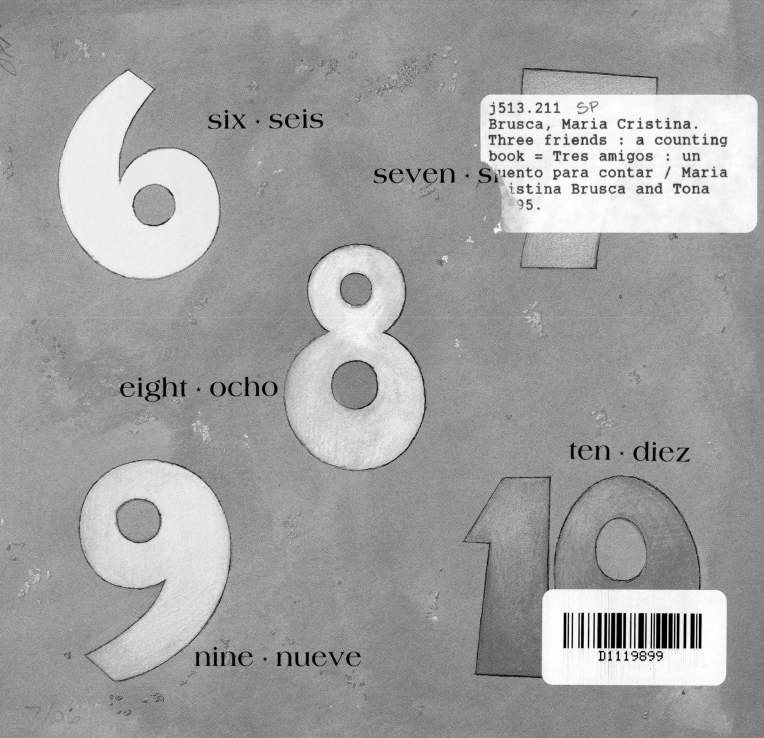

six · seis

seven · siete

eight · ocho

nine · nueve

ten · diez

To our three friends,
George, Donna, and Shuggie

A nuestros tres amigos,
George, Donna y Shuggie

Henry Holt and Company, LLC, *Publishers since 1866*
115 West 18th Street, New York, New York 10011

Henry Holt is a registered trademark of Henry Holt and Company, LLC

Text copyright © 1995 by María Cristina Brusca and Tona Wilson
Illustrations copyright © 1995 by María Cristina Brusca
All rights reserved.
Published in Canada by Fitzhenry & Whiteside Ltd.,
195 Allstate Parkway, Markham, Ontario L3R 4T8.

Library of Congress Cataloging-in-Publication Data
Brusca, María Cristina.
Three friends: a counting book = Tres amigos: un cuento para
contar / by/por María Cristina Brusca and Tona Wilson;
illustrated by/ilustrado por María Cristina Brusca.
1. Counting—Juvenile literature. [1. Counting.
2. Spanish language materials—Bilingual.] I. Wilson, Tona.
II. Title.   III. Title: Tres amigos.   IV. Title: 3 friends.
QA113.B787   1995   513.2'11—dc20   [E]   94-44648

ISBN 0-8050-3707-1
First Edition—1995
Printed in Mexico
3   5   7   9   10   8   6   4   2

The artist used watercolor and ink on Windsor & Newton
paper to prepare the illustrations for this book.

THREE FRIENDS ★ TRES AMIGOS

A Counting Book
Un cuento para contar

María Cristina Brusca and Tona Wilson
illustrated by/ilustrado por María Cristina Brusca

Henry Holt and Company
New York

Un caballo

One horse

Dos vaqueros

Two cowboys

Tres amigos

Three friends

Cuatro armadillos

Four armadillos

Cinco vacas

Five cows

Seis plantas rodadoras

Six tumbleweeds

Siete correcaminos

Seven roadrunners

Ocho coyotes

Eight coyotes

Nueve serpientes

Nine snakes

Diez cactos

Ten cactuses

Nueve serpientes saltan.

Nine snakes jump.

Ocho coyotes cantan.

Eight coyotes sing.

Siete correcaminos corren.

Seven roadrunners run.

Seis plantas rodadoras ruedan.

Six tumbleweeds tumble.

Cinco vacas escapan.

Five cows escape.

Cuatro armadillos ríen.

Four armadillos laugh.

Tres amigos comen.

Three friends eat.

Dos vaqueros duermen.

Two cowboys sleep.

Una luna brilla.

One moon shines.

Fried egg · Huevo frito

Horse · Caballo

Frying pan · Sartén

Wagon · Carreta

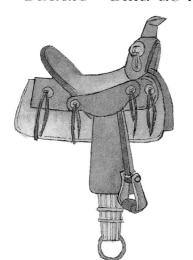

Coffeepot · Cafetera

Saddle · Silla de montar

Brand · Marca

Horse shoe · Herradura

Branding iron · Hierro de marcar

Lasso · Lazo

Hat · Sombrero

Gloves · Guantes

Cowboy · Vaquero

Cowgirl · Vaquera

Chaps · Chaparreras

Boots · Botas

Spur · Espuela

ten · diez

nine · nueve

eight · ocho

six · seis

seven · siete